South Asian Americans

Scott Ingram

Curriculum Consultant: Michael Koren,
Social Studies Teacher, Maple Dale School, Fox Point, Wisconsin

WORLD ALMANAC® LIBRARY

Please visit our web site at: www.garethstevens.com
For a free color catalog describing World Almanac® Library's list of
high-quality books and multimedia programs, call 1-800-848-2928 (USA)
or 1-800-387-3178 (Canada). World Almanac® Library's fax: (414) 332-3567.

Library of Congress Cataloging-in-Publication Data

Ingram, Scott.
    South Asian Americans / by Scott Ingram.
        p. cm. – (World Almanac Library of American immigration)
    Includes bibliographical references and index.
    ISBN-10: 0-8368-7318-1 – ISBN-13: 978-0-8368-7318-4 (lib. bdg.)
    ISBN-10: 0-8368-7331-9 – ISBN-13: 978-0-8368-7331-3 (softcover)
    1. South Asian Americans–History–Juvenile literature. 2. South Asian
Americans–Social conditions–Juvenile literature. 3. Immigrants–United
States–History–Juvenile literature. 4. South Asia–Emigration and
immigration–History–Juvenile literature. 5. United States–Emigration
and immigration–History–Juvenile literature. I. Title. II. Series.
    E184.S69I54   2007
    973'.004914–dc22   2006005391

First published in 2007 by
World Almanac® Library
A member of the WRC Media Family of Companies
330 West Olive Street, Suite 100
Milwaukee, WI 53212, USA

Produced by Discovery Books
Editor: Sabrina Crewe
Designer and page production: Sabine Beaupré
Photo researcher: Sabrina Crewe
Maps and diagrams: Stefan Chabluk
Consultant: Vinodh Kutty
World Almanac® Library editorial direction: Mark J. Sachner
World Almanac® Library editor: Barbara Kiely Miller
World Almanac® Library art direction: Tammy West
World Almanac® Library production: Jessica Morris

Picture credits: Darpana Athale: 35; The Bancroft Library, University of California,
Berkeley: 28; CORBIS: cover, title page, 5, 8, 9, 10, 11, 19, 21, 30, 31, 32, 33, 34, 37,
39, 40, 41, 43; Holt-Atherton Special Collections, University of the Pacific Library: 25;
Kleiner Perkins Caulfield & Byers: 36; Library of Congress: 24, 29; Punjabi American
Heritage Society: 27; San Francisco History Center, San Francisco Library: 17;
Southern Oregon Historical Society: 22; Vancouver Public Library, Special
Collections: 13, 16.

Printed in the United States of America

1 2 3 4 5 6 7 8 9 10 09 08 07 06

Contents

Front cover: A 2004 parade in New York City celebrates New Year in the Sikh religion. Many of the first South Asian immigrants were Sikhs, and today there are Sikh communities in several U.S. cities.

Title page: Among Hindus around the world, the most important festival is Diwali, celebrated here in a temple in Philadelphia, Pennsylvania. Hindus in the United States observe the holiday with worship, lighting lamps, visiting relatives, feasting, and setting off fireworks.

Introduction

The United States has often been called "a nation of immigrants." With the exception of Native Americans— who have inhabited North America for thousands of years— all Americans can trace their roots to other parts of the world.

Immigration is not a thing of the past. More than seventy million people came to the United States between 1820 and 2005. One-fifth of that total—about fourteen million people—immigrated since the start of 1990. Overall, more people have immigrated permanently to the United States than to any other single nation.

Push and Pull

Historians write of the "push" and "pull" factors that lead people to emigrate. "Push" factors are the conditions in the homeland that convince people to leave. Many immigrants to the United States were—and still are—fleeing persecution or poverty. "Pull" factors are those that attract people to settle in another country. The dream of freedom or jobs or both continues to pull immigrants to the United States. People from many countries around the world view the United States as a place of opportunity.

> "Desi . . . it means Indians, Pakistanis, Bangladeshis . . . but I don't see separation, I see unity. When we use the word desi it brings us all together."
>
> *Vijay Prashad, a South Asian American living in New York City, 2000*

Building a Nation

Immigrants to the United States have not always found what they expected. People worked long hours for little pay, often doing jobs that others did not want to do. Many groups also endured prejudice.

In spite of these challenges, immigrants and their children built the United States of America, from its farms, railroads, and computer industries to its beliefs and traditions. They have enriched

▲ A Pakistani American, holding his three-year-old grandson, celebrates Pakistan's independence day with a Pakistani flag and a U.S. flag.

American life with their culture and ideas. Although they honor their heritage, most immigrants and their descendants are proud to call themselves Americans first and foremost.

Coming from South Asia

Among the immigrants who have come to the United States are people from the nations of South Asia. Most South Asian immigrants to the United States have come from India. This book is also about Americans from Pakistan, Bangladesh, and Sri Lanka.

Between 1899 and 1920, about seven thousand South Asians arrived on the West Coast. Between 1947 and 1965, another sixty-four hundred South Asians immigrated to the United States. This second wave comprised mostly relatives of the first wave of immigrants. In 1965, the third wave of South Asian immigration began. This was the largest wave, and it is continuing today.

People of the Land

Today, more than 2.6 million people of South Asian descent are estimated to live in the United States, and aspects of their culture are now familiar in mainstream U.S. life. Whatever their country of origin, South Asian Americans generally overlook national differences when they settle in the United States. They use the term *desi* to describe themselves. Taken from India's Hindi language, desi means person of the land. Desis have become one of the most successful immigrant groups to enter the United States in recent years.

CHAPTER 1

Life in the Homeland

The Indian subcontinent is a triangular landmass that extends south from the Himalaya Mountains to the Indian Ocean. Two of the world's longest rivers flow from the Himalayas across the subcontinent—the Indus River and the Ganges River.

An Ancient Civilization

In ancient times, one of the world's most advanced civilizations formed in the Indus River valley. The first branch of medicine—the Ayurveda system—developed in India between three thousand and five thousand years ago.

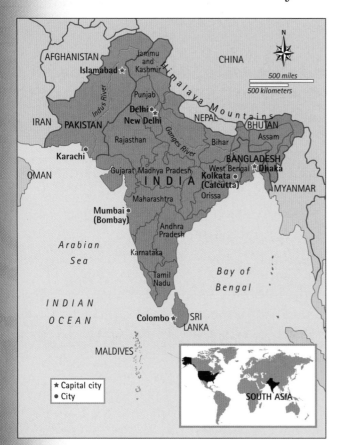

◀ The South Asian nations covered in this book—India, Pakistan, Bangladesh, and Sri Lanka—are shown on this map. India got its name from its location along the Indus River in what is now Pakistan but was once part of India. Bangladesh was also once in India—it formed part of the Indian state of Bengal. Bangladesh became a region of Pakistan when India was divided into two nations, India and Pakistan, in 1947. Bangladesh finally became an independent nation in 1971. The island of Sri Lanka, once known as Ceylon, became a nation in 1948.

For centuries, the huge subcontinent was known as India or Hindustan. Today, the region is known as South Asia, and it is divided into several countries. The largest are India, Pakistan, and Bangladesh. Two other nations, Nepal and Bhutan, lie in the Himalayas. Two island nations in the Indian Ocean are also part of South Asia—Sri Lanka and Maldives. Some people consider Afghanistan to be part of South Asia, too.

Hindus, Sikhs, and Buddhists

Indian culture embraces several of the world's most important religions. Hinduism originated in India more than five thousand years ago. On the Indian subcontinent, more than three out of four people practice Hinduism.

One faith that developed from Hinduism was known as Sikhism. The word *sikh* means learner. The Sikhs (pronounced with two syllables: Seh-iks) broke away from Hinduism in part because they refused to accept the caste system of the Hindus. Sikhs believe that a man's beard and hair should never be cut. They also believe hair should be kept covered, so male Sikhs wear cloth turbans wrapped around the head. Sikhism originated in the northwestern Indian state of Punjab, where most people are farmers. Most Sikhs adopt the last name Singh, which means lion in Punjabi.

In about 500 B.C., Hindu prince Siddartha Gautama created another of the world's largest religions, Buddhism. Most Buddhists in South Asia today are in Sri Lanka, Bhutan, and Nepal.

Caste System

According to Hindu belief, each person is born into one of four castes, or levels of society. From top to bottom, the levels are: Brahmins, the religious leaders and teachers; Kshatriyas, or military leaders; Vaishyas, farmers and merchants; and Sudras, the peasants and servants. In addition, a large group was known as the Dalits, or Untouchables—these people were historically considered the lowest level of society. For much of India's history, even into modern times, a person's caste determined what professions he or she could choose. Marriages usually took place within the same caste. Rules prohibited people of different castes from even socializing with each other.

Islam and the Mughal Empire

The Muslim religion, Islam, originated in the Middle East and spread to northern India during the two-hundred-year period of the Mughal Empire, which became the most powerful empire in Asia in the 1500s. Although the Mughal Empire helped to spread Islam, its first rulers actually encouraged religious freedom. During this time, Indian Muslims and Hindus developed the classical music of India. Much of what Americans consider Indian food was also developed during the Mughal period, as was the architecture that is world famous today.

▲ From the 1600s to colonial times, India was ruled by many maharajahs. In this traditional Indian painting, the Maharajah Sher Singh is shown on horseback. The Indus River is visible in the background.

A British Colony

Eventually, violence broke out between Muslims and Hindus, and the Mughal Empire declined. By the late 1600s, India was an enormous land with hundreds of small kingdoms ruled by kings known as maharajahs. European colonists, meanwhile, arrived to exploit India's resources. The subcontinent became a colony of Britain, with its capital at Calcutta (now Kolkata).

Like American colonists before the American Revolution, the people of India wanted independence. In 1885, the Indian National Congress (INC) was established. Most of its members were educated, English-speaking Hindus who wanted India to be self-ruling.

In 1906, Muslims in India formed an organization similar to the INC called the Muslim League. For the first decades of the 1900s, members of these two organizations called for India's independence. Tension between the two religious groups, however, remained high. In 1940, the Muslim League demanded that in addition to independence, a separate Muslim country should be created from Indian lands. The Hindu nation would keep the name India; the Muslim nation would be called Pakistan.

Independence and Partition

In 1947, Britain granted independence to India. The subcontinent was divided into the mostly Hindu nation of India and the mostly Muslim Pakistan. Pakistan was one nation divided into two parts—West and East Pakistan—separated by about 1,000 miles (1,600 kilometers) of Indian territory. Part of Bengal (or Bangla, as it was known in the Bengali language) was separated from India to form East Pakistan. Similarly, part of Punjab ended up in West Pakistan.

In the greatest mass migration in history, Muslims left India, and Hindus and Sikhs moved to India from Pakistan. The states of Punjab and Bengal, divided by the new national borders, suffered enormous upheaval. The state of Kashmir became a battleground, with neither country willing to give up control of the region.

The effects of the partition of India continued for many years. West Pakistan held Pakistan's capital city (first Karachi and then Islamabad) and much of its wealth. East Pakistan's Bengali leaders demanded independence for their poverty-stricken, overcrowded region. In response, Pakistani troops invaded East Pakistan. After much violence and loss of life, Indian

"The . . . fire from cannons, machine guns, and automatics continued throughout the night. On the morning of the 26th, the Pakistani [troops] began to go through the halls and apartments. . . . Those unfortunate students who had failed to flee were all killed by the Pakistanis. This is how we spent thirty-six hours. When, on the morning of the 27th, the so-called curfew was lifted, I left forever."

Rafiquil Islam, Bangladeshi American, describing a 1971 attack on a college campus in Bangladesh, 2005

▶ Mohandas Karamchand Gandhi (1869–1948) led India to independence through nonviolent protest. His approach greatly influenced the U.S. civil rights movement of the 1950s and 1960s. Known as Mahatma, meaning "great soul," Ghandi (*right*) is shown here at a 1942 conference with Jawaharlal Nehru (*left*), who later became India's first prime minister.

forces entered East Pakistan to protect the Bengalis, and the Pakistani troops retreated. The new nation of Bangladesh was formed from East Pakistan in 1971.

Sri Lanka

The island nation of Sri Lanka, located about 60 miles (100 km) off the southeast coast of India, was originally settled by people from the Indian subcontinent. The Tamils, who are mainly Hindu, live in the northern section of the island. The Sinhalese, who are largely Buddhist, live in the south. British colonists took control of the island, then called Ceylon, in 1796 and developed coffee, tea, and rubber plantations. In 1948, Ceylon was granted its independence by Britain, and the nation changed its name to Sri Lanka in 1972. Tension between the Sinhalese and Tamils erupted into war in 1983. Tens of thousands of people have died in the long-running civil war. The violence has been largely responsible for the emigration of Sri Lankans to the United States.

▲ Sri Lankan women and children take refuge in a temple after a huge tsunami hit the island in 2004. Already hard hit by civil war, coastal areas of Sri Lanka were devastated by the tsunami.

Sikhs of Punjab

From the late 1800s until modern times, the turbulent events in South Asia gave many people reason to leave their homelands. In the late 1800s, many Sikhs from the state of Punjab left for two main reasons. A drought in northwest India destroyed vast areas of farmland in Punjab. In addition, many Sikhs had joined the British army or British colonial police. Their service to the British made the Sikhs unpopular with Hindus and Muslims who sought independence. That tension, as well as the loss of their farmland to the drought, caused about seven thousand people to leave India for North America in the first wave of emigration. In that period, the Sikhs' destination was usually Canada, which at the time was part of the British Empire.

▲ The nation of Bangladesh was founded in 1971 when it broke away from Pakistan. Formerly the eastern part of the Indian state of Bengal, Bangladesh suffers from poverty and frequent natural disasters.

Fleeing Violence and Overcrowding

Tension between different groups continued to be the main reason for leaving South Asia. The second wave of South Asians left the subcontinent during the 1940s because of the violence that resulted from the partition of India.

The third and largest wave of South Asians who emigrated to the United States came after 1965. There were many reasons to leave. The caste system, although officially banned in 1949, still limited the opportunities of many Hindus. Wars and terrorism affected large areas. The economies of India and Pakistan were slow to recover from the violent upheaval of the 1940s. In addition, South Asia had become the most densely populated region in the world.

In India, starvation, poverty, and housing shortages overwhelmed government resources. Millions of Bengalis had fled to refugee camps around Calcutta in 1971. Their numbers added to the burden of the Indian government.

Today, Bangladesh is still one of the two or three poorest nations in the world, overcrowded and often ravaged by floods. Life-threatening diseases, such as malaria, are widespread and have resulted in a life expectancy of just over fifty years.

Pakistan has suffered difficulties as well. Afghanistan, on Pakistan's western border, has gone through years of war involving foreign countries and religious extremists. This fighting has frequently spilled into Pakistan.

"The breaking point for me came when my eleven-year-old son came home from school one day talking about the Kalishnikov [assault rifle] that he and his friends had been playing with."

Waris Khan, who came to New York City from an area of western Pakistan where fighting between Afghanis had spilled across the border, 1997

CHAPTER 2

Emigration

In the late 1800s, the first wave of emigration from South Asia to North America—mostly to Canada—began. Approximately seven thousand South Asians who had made the journey from India then entered the United States between 1900 and 1920.

Leaving Punjab
Many of the Punjabi Sikhs who left India in this period sold land to pay for their long trip or were helped by money from relatives. Leaving their villages, the emigrants traveled first by train. They headed southeast across much of the subcontinent to the crowded, humid port of Calcutta. There, emigrants boarded steamships that carried them on a twelve-day journey to Hong Kong. From there, another ship carried them across the Pacific Ocean for the eighteen-day trip to the west coast of North America.

Students from Calcutta
A smaller group of the first wave made a similar journey from India. They were English-speaking students who left India to study in American universities. They were encouraged to emigrate by the INC, which published articles urging students to go abroad to work for India's independence. Most of these students were already at colleges in Calcutta, where the INC was based.

Immigration Limits
The early 1920s was a period of strong anti-immigrant feeling in the United States. U.S. immigration laws of 1917 and 1924 barred the immigration of people from Asia, and hardly any South Asians emigrated to the United States for more than twenty years.

In the 1920s, however, there were about seventy-five hundred South Asian Americans already in the United States. Some of these immigrants belonged to organizations that were working to gain

▲ The earliest Punjabi Sikh emigrants traveled to Canada first and then migrated to the United States. This picture from the early 1900s shows a group of new arrivals from India at the port in Vancouver, Canada.

India's independence. By 1946, these groups had convinced U.S. political leaders that a free India would be an important ally of the United States. In 1946, Congress responded by passing a law, the Luce-Cellar Act, that allowed two hundred South Asian immigrants into the United States each year. After India and Pakistan became separate countries in 1947, the quota was divided into one hundred for each of the two nations.

The Second Wave

Even after 1946, emigration from South Asia to the United States remained very limited for the next twenty years. The 1946 law, however, did allow South Asians in the United States to become U.S. citizens through the process of naturalization. South Asian Americans who had become U.S. citizens could then bring relatives to the United States. This change allowed the extended families of many South Asian Americans to emigrate.

Some U.S. citizens returned to South Asia to gather their relatives. Others sent money home to pay for their families' passage to the United States. It was a time of violence and upheaval across India and Pakistan, however. Travel by train—the main form of transportation across the vast subcontinent—was dangerous. Some regions of Punjab and Bengal were war zones. Emigrants had to make their way to Calcutta through crowds of people displaced by the conflict. In all, only about sixty-four hundred South Asians managed to emigrate to the United States between 1946 and 1965.

The Third Wave Begins

In 1965, a new law completely changed U.S. immigration. Before that year, immigration had been limited to certain races and certain countries. The Immigration and Nationality Act of 1965 allowed a total of 290,000 people into the United States each year on a first-come, first-serve basis. The racial limits were abandoned. There was a limit of 20,000 people from a single country, but relatives of U.S. citizens were not part of that total.

The raised quota meant that thousands of South Asians could come to the United States, become naturalized, and, in turn, bring in their family members. The trip became much easier, too. By the 1960s, emigrants could travel by airplane. They arrived in the United States to begin new lives after a journey that took only hours rather than the weeks traveling by ship had taken.

Indian and Pakistani Emigration

The great flood of people leaving South Asia began. By the early 1970s, thousands of the best-educated members of India's middle class were emigrating, largely because of the warfare, economic depression, crowding, and poverty. Educated Pakistanis, also weary of their living conditions and constant warfare, were leaving, too.

A part of the 1965 law that attracted immigrants from both India and Pakistan was a special allowance for admitting those who had college degrees or training in certain fields. One of those fields was medicine. In South Asia, doctors and other health care professionals were limited in their job choices and in their salaries. People with training in engineering or business also had nowhere to look for work. All these professionals were encouraged to come to the United States.

Emigrants from Bangladesh and Sri Lanka

By 1972, Bangladesh and Sri Lanka had become separate nations and were each permitted a quota of twenty thousand emigrants to the United States. In the 1980s, Bangladeshis joined the wave of emigration from South Asia. After 1983, the civil war in Sri Lanka drove many Sri Lankans, especially those who were educated English speakers, to leave the war-torn island nation.

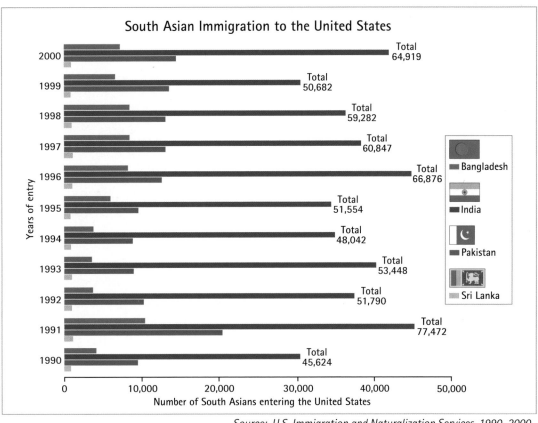

South Asian Immigration to the United States

Year	Total
2000	Total 64,919
1999	Total 50,682
1998	Total 59,282
1997	Total 60,847
1996	Total 66,876
1995	Total 51,554
1994	Total 48,042
1993	Total 53,448
1992	Total 51,790
1991	Total 77,472
1990	Total 45,624

Years of entry

Number of South Asians entering the United States: 0, 10,000, 20,000, 30,000, 40,000, 50,000

Legend: Bangladesh, India, Pakistan, Sri Lanka

Source: U.S. Immigration and Naturalization Services, 1990–2000

▲ After 1990, South Asians began to enter the United States on H1-B visas. This chart shows the numbers of immigrants who came in the years 1990–2000 from the South Asian nations discussed in this book. In 2000, there were an estimated 116,000 unauthorized U.S. residents—people without visas or U.S. citizenship—from these nations.

Special Visas

In 1990, the Immigration Reform and Control Act raised the total number of immigrants allowed into the United States to seven hundred thousand a year. A key part of the 1990 law was the creation of a new visa called the H-1B. The visa is a three-year permit given to skilled workers in fields that include engineering, education, business, law, computer technology, and the performing arts.

The law allows thousands of H-1B visas to be issued in addition to the annual immigrant quota. A U.S. employer must sponsor workers entering under H-1B visas. Some immigrants are already in the United States under student visas, and sponsors help them make the switch to H-1Bs. An H-1B worker is allowed to renew the visa once. After six years, he or she can apply for permanent resident status—otherwise known as a green card. This step begins the process of becoming a naturalized citizen. In recent years, the opportunities offered by the H-1B visa have attracted many workers with computer skills to come to the United States from South Asia.

CHAPTER 3

Arriving in the United States

O n April 6, 1899, the *San Francisco Chronicle* newspaper ran a small article with the headline "Sikhs Permitted to Land." The article described the arrival of four Sikh men in California and stated that one man "speaks English with fluency."

The First Arrivals

This announcement is generally considered the first mention of South Asian immigrants arriving in the United States. Although some South Asians who came to the United States at the turn of the twentieth century were Hindus and Muslims, most were Sikhs from Punjab. In most cases, the Punjabis had intended to settle in Canada. They were not welcomed by Canadian workers, however, who did not want to compete with immigrants for jobs. These anti-immigrant attitudes

◀ Many early South Asian immigrants came to the United States from Canada, where they had faced prejudice in the lumber industries of the Pacific Northwest. This group of workers was photographed at the North Pacific Lumber Company in British Columbia between 1900 and 1910.

▲ Angel Island, shown here in 1939, was the main U.S. entry point for early South Asian immigrants. The handwriting of Sikhs waiting to be granted entry is still visible on the walls of the detention dormitories. The immigration station is now a museum.

led Canada's government to ban immigration by all South Asians in 1908. Many Punjabis made their way from Canada to the United States. After 1908, Punjabis also began to come directly to the United States from India, arriving on the West Coast.

Angel Island

Beginning in 1910, all Asian immigrants arriving on the West Coast were required to enter the United States through the Angel Island immigration station in San Francisco Bay, California. At Angel Island, Indian immigrants were separated from Japanese and Filipino immigrants, and men were separated from women and children. All immigrants were given complete medical exams. In some cases, evidence of a childhood disease—pockmarks or scars— were enough to have an immigrant deported.

After examination, the immigrants were assigned to detention dormitories that were little more than prison buildings. There, they awaited questioning by the Board of Special Inquiry concerning their plans. During this time, immigrants lived like prisoners. Living conditions were terrible, and the food was barely edible. Hazara Singh, who arrived at Angel Island in 1913, told his great-granddaughters that living in the dormitories was like "living in a horse stable." The wait for interrogation often lasted weeks.

Unwelcome in America

During this period, South Asian Americans were classified as resident aliens. Resident aliens were granted many of the same rights as U.S. citizens, such as freedom of speech and religion, but U.S.

Bhagat Singh Thind

In 1923, the U.S. Supreme Court heard a case brought by Bhagat Singh Thind, a Punjabi who had come to the United States in 1913 and worked at a lumber mill to earn money for college. When the United States entered World War I in 1917, Thind joined the U.S. Army. He received an honorable discharge in 1918. In 1920, Thind applied for citizenship and was approved by the U.S. District Court. The Bureau of Naturalization, however, claimed that under U.S. law at the time, only "white" people could become citizens. Immigrants from the Indian subcontinent had been classified as Asian, which made them ineligible. Thind claimed that he, like all people from South Asia, was not Asian but Caucasian. The Supreme Court, however, agreed with the Bureau of Naturalization that Caucasians were not necessarily white: "The physical group characteristics of the Hindus render them readily distinguishable from the various groups of persons in this country commonly recognized as white." It was a discouraging event for South Asian immigrants. Thind, however, remained in the United States, completed his studies, and gained U.S. citizenship a few years later through the state of New York.

laws of the period denied all Asians—including South Asians— an important right that was given to European aliens: Asian immigrants were not allowed to become U.S. citizens.

Most white Americans knew little about India or Sikhism. In the first two decades of the twentieth century, immigrants from India endured the same prejudice that was shown toward other Asian Americans. In 1905, the Asiatic Exclusion League (AEL) was formed in California to prevent more Asians—Japanese, Korean, Filipino, and Indian—from coming to the United States. The AEL also wanted to make Asian Americans leave the country. In the case of South Asians, the AEL members spread rumors about "Hindoos" that accused them of carrying deadly diseases. An AEL leaflet called them the "most undesirable of all the Asiatic races."

Arriving in the Second Wave

Between 1947 and 1965, about seven thousand immigrants from India and fifteen hundred immigrants from Pakistan arrived in the United States. This wave of immigrants included relatives of South

Asians who had, at last, been allowed to become naturalized U.S. citizens. It also included the new wives of Punjabi men who had returned to Punjab from the United States to marry women from their region. The majority of immigrants in the second wave joined Punjabi Americans in central California. Unlike earlier arrivals, the newcomers were often accepted in the small towns where they settled because their predecessors were now part of the communities.

After 1965

Over the following decades, as the largest wave of South Asian immigrants entered the United States, South Asian communities spread beyond California. Between 1965 and 1975, more than ninety thousand professionals and their families flew into New York City. Often, men came first. As well as doctors, more than twenty thousand engineers from South Asia came to work in U.S. companies. They then sent for their wives and children. More than fifty thousand family members eventually joined the immigrant men.

For the first time, South Asians became a presence on the East Coast. From an estimated population of fifteen thousand people of South Asian descent in the United States in 1960, the South Asian American population grew to more than two million by the time of

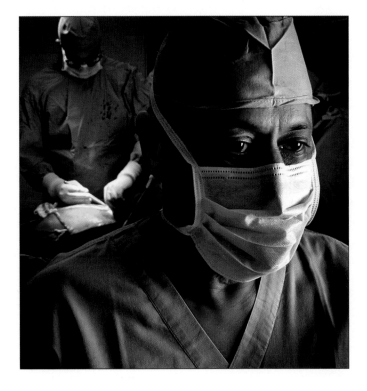

◀ After 1965, many South Asian doctors arrived in the United States hoping to find opportunities unavailable in their homelands. Dr. Naresh Trehan, shown here in 2003, arrived in 1969 and was earning $1.5 million a year as a heart surgeon by the mid-1980s. He returned to India, however, when he realized his skills were desperately needed there. Trehan now works in New Delhi.

South Asian Culture in the United States

South Asians entering the United States in the late 1960s and early 1970s arrived at a time when South Asian cultures—especially that of India—had become familiar to many Americans. Many people had developed an interest in Hindu and Buddhist teachings. Such practices as meditation and yoga began to spread to areas of the U.S. The word *guru*—a word from the Hindi language meaning guide or teacher—made its way into American English. Indian culture became especially popular among young people during the 1960s. Although few South Asian Americans were themselves part of this movement, American awareness of their culture made it easier for arriving immigrants.

"At the time . . . there were no opportunities in India. The . . . opportunities were not there. . . . The U.S. lets people . . . start their own companies and start their own ideas. . . . It's the land of opportunity, and I don't think anyone can match it."

N. Sivakumar, who came to the United States to work as a software designer in 1998 and plans to become a naturalized citizen, 2005

the U.S. census in 2000. Today, there are probably 2.6 to 2.8 million South Asian Americans.

Acceptance and Other Advantages

South Asian immigrants arriving after the late 1960s experienced much more acceptance of their culture than earlier arrivals had found. The later arrivals had other advantages, too. Almost all immigrants spoke some English, and many had received a high-quality education. Because of these factors, South Asian immigrants quickly found jobs, not only in health care but in business and in higher education. Women with a college education, who may not have had equal opportunities in South Asia, were able to find jobs in hospitals, schools, and private businesses.

Arriving After 1990

After 1990, many more Bangladeshis, Sri Lankans, and Pakistanis settled in New York City and surrounding areas on the East Coast. These newcomers were not as well off and professionally qualified as the South Asians who had arrived in the 1970s. They began to fill jobs in service industries, such as hotels, restaurants, service stations, and transportation.

At the same time, the introduction of

▲ In a 2005 ceremony at the former immigration station on New York City's Ellis Island, Pakistani American Mohammed Mustafa becomes a U.S. citizen. South Asians and other immigrants have to live and work in the United States for several years and take a citizenship test before they can become citizens.

H-1B visas allowed U.S. employers to hire skilled professionals from South Asia. This was especially true in the field of computer manufacturing and software design. The creation of the H-1B visa occurred at a time when there were large numbers of South Asians who had degrees in computer science but few opportunities in their homelands. Thousands of H-1B workers arrived in the United States from South Asia during the 1990s.

Landing with $100

When Dr. C. T. Nanavati landed at Kennedy Airport, New York, in 1975, he had $100 in his pocket. Trained as a veterinarian in India, he learned that he would need another year of training before he could obtain a veterinary license in the United States. When Nanavati was finally licensed to start his vet practice, he had only enough money to rent a former hot dog stand for an office. "In the beginning, it was very hard. I didn't have money for anything, not even eating." To support himself, Nanavati worked in a factory during the day and only opened his "office" from 6:00 P.M. until midnight. As the only South Asian in a small Connecticut town, he worked hard to gain people's trust. He often accepted food from people who could not afford to pay for the care he provided for their animals. Eventually, Nanavati moved to a real office. Today, he owns two veterinary practices.

CHAPTER 4

Farmers and Students

In the early 1900s, many South Asians who had originally arrived in Canada decided to come south to the United States in search of warmer weather and better jobs. By the 1910s, several thousand men from Punjab were working on the U.S. West Coast, mainly in California. A large number of South Asians—Hindus and Muslims as well as Sikhs—found their first jobs working on the railroads and in the lumber industries of the Pacific Coast.

Migrant Farm Workers

The Punjabi Sikhs, however, were farmers, and farming prospects eventually drew them toward California's Central Valley. There, the landscape was similar to Punjab, and few white Americans in the

▼ Hardworking Sikhs found jobs in railroad construction when they first came to the West Coast in the early 1900s. This group was photographed in about 1909 working on the Pacific and Eastern Railroad.

region were competing for the available work.

At first, the men worked as migrant farm laborers. Groups of ten to twelve workers traveled from farm to farm, following the planting or harvesting cycle. The Punjabis worked in the orchards, vineyards, and sugar beet fields of the Sacramento Valley in the northern part of the state. Then they moved south to the vineyards and citrus groves of the San Joaquin Valley in central California.

One man was hired to cook traditional Punjabi foods for each group. Since most of the men spoke just Punjabi, a group usually depended on a leader, or "boss man," who was fluent in English. The boss man would serve as their spokesperson with white farm owners. In most cases, the boss men had served in the British military and had some Western education.

Land in California

Punjabi Americans quickly built a reputation as hard workers, which enabled them to obtain loans to buy or lease land. In 1913, however, California passed its first statewide anti-Asian law—the Webb-Hartley Law, also called the Alien Land Law. The law said that "aliens ineligible to citizenship" could rent land for only three years. It barred aliens from

The Bellingham Riots

Among the South Asian Americans who found work in the Pacific Northwest were several hundred men who settled in Bellingham, Washington, in the early 1900s. Anti-immigrant feelings stirred up by the AEL had begun to influence American workers of European descent. They were led to believe that workers from India would take their jobs because they were willing to work for lower wages. On September 4, 1907, anti-immigrant feelings boiled over into violence. Speakers on street corners made speeches, demanding that the people of Bellingham "drive out the cheap labor."

Soon, a mob of several hundred white workers descended on the ramshackle houses along Bellingham's waterfront where the Indians rented rooms. Many of the immigrants were pulled from their rooms and beaten in the street. Some fled with only the clothes on their backs. Those not directly driven out by the mob left the next day by train, boat, or on foot. The incident drew wide attention to Bellingham. Newspaper editorials, including one in the *San Francisco Chronicle*, criticized the mob actions, but most supported the need for a "white West Coast," as the *Chronicle* put it. The Bellingham Riots were the first of several such attacks on South Asian Americans in the first two decades of the 1900s.

▲ Migrant farm workers and other agricultural laborers lived in poor conditions in the farming regions of California. This 1935 photo shows housing for workers in the Imperial Valley. South Asian American families improved their lives and prospects by leasing their own land and farming for themselves.

purchasing any land in the future. Although the law did not mention them by name, "aliens ineligible to citizenship" referred to Asian Americans.

By 1920, in spite of the law, Punjabi Americans owned 2,099 acres (850 hectares) of land and leased an additional 86,340 acres (34,940 ha). Most of this land was in the Sacramento and San Joaquin Valleys. Punjabi American farmers had also moved farther south to an area that had long been considered almost impossible to farm because it lacked water—the Imperial Valley.

The Imperial Valley, located close to the Mexican border, had been desert for centuries. In the early 1900s, however, water from the Colorado River was diverted across the valley to supply drinking water for Los Angeles. A short time later, Punjabis began to arrive in the valley as they worked their way south. They leased thousands of acres of land in the Imperial Valley. They used water from the Colorado River for irrigation and also applied farming methods they had developed in drought-stricken Punjab.

Punjabi-Mexican Marriages

Word of the available land spread, and many Punjabis moved to the Imperial Valley. Most of these men had come to the United States as bachelors. Many had intended to earn enough money in North America and then return to Punjab and buy land. As conditions worsened in India, however, and they achieved some success in farming, they decided to stay permanently in California.

Over the years, Punjabi Americans in California became more prosperous, and many wanted to marry and have families. Before 1946, U.S. immigration laws would not permit them to bring brides from India to the United States. Laws also prohibited intermarriage between certain races—since Americans of Indian descent were classified as Asians, they could not marry whites. They were, however, permitted to marry Mexican American women.

In the 1920s, many Punjabi Americans—more than two thousand—and other South Asian Americans married women of Mexican descent. These marriages helped those who owned land avoid the problems created by the Alien Land Law. Many of the Mexican American women were naturalized U.S. citizens, so the land leases or ownership could be put in their names. In addition, children born to these couples were U.S. citizens by law. Some Punjabi Americans put the land deeds in their children's names.

"When I met Susanna, she did sewing . . . she cut all the kids' hair, she made all their clothes. . . . I found Susanna in 1937, and then everything got good. Susanna . . . didn't want to buy anything; she only wanted to buy groceries. She chopped cotton, she worked, and she didn't even want to buy a dress. I went to the store, I bought her a dress."

Punjabi American Moola Singh, who married Mexican American Susanna Mesa Rodriguez in 1937, speaking in 1985

Religious Centers

The first Hindu temple in the United States was built in San Francisco, California. The first Muslim mosque for South Asian Americans was in Sacramento, California. The majority of South Asian Americans, however, were Sikhs, and the center of community life in most South Asian communities were the *gurdwaras*, or Sikh temples. The first gurdwara was built in Stockton, California.

At community meetings or religious services held in the gurdwaras, men and women sat in separate areas, which was the custom in India. The men generally spoke Punjabi at meetings, but the women spoke English—few of the women at the temple were Punjabi.

▶ Sikh Americans gather outside the gurdwara in Stockton, California, in about 1920.

"My dad came to the [Imperial] Valley and . . . had a modest farm . . . people respected him. . . . Not only the people in the Valley, but also his own people, whether they were Hindu, whether they were Sikh, whether they were Muslim. . . . My father from the very beginning understood that there was no place to worship in his religion. There was no mosque, so he never really put pressure on my mother to teach us to follow the Muslim faith. The most convenient was naturally my mother's faith, which was Catholic . . . so we have the Mohameds who are very good Catholics."

Niaz Mohamed, Jr., whose father Niaz married Lydia Garcia and raised five children on a farm in the Imperial Valley, 2000

Family Life

For many Mexican American women who married Americans from India, cultural differences created problems. According to Punjabi custom, the women were responsible not only for the household chores for their husbands, but also for any unmarried men who worked with their husbands. They often cooked, washed, and cleaned for several men who lived in their homes or nearby.

Following Indian custom, sons or other male relatives usually received any inheritance. The children of Indian-Mexican marriages were often raised in the mother's faith, however, which among Mexican Americans was usually Catholicism. Children who grew up in the Punjabi-Mexican community most often married partners who had also grown up in the community. Today, there are many families in the agricultural regions of California whose names reflect their combined South Asian and Mexican heritages.

Students from India

The first wave of arrivals to the United States also included young men who were pulled to the United States for political and educational reasons. They were from relatively prosperous families and were fluent in English. Most were also dedicated to India's independence. They came to the United States for education and to build an independence movement outside of India. In the first years of the twentieth century, Indian student groups formed at the University of Washington in Seattle, Washington, and at the University of California at Berkeley, California. The students lived in rooming houses near college campuses.

▲ Punjabi Americans and Punjabi-Mexican Americans maintain a strong presence in several California communities. This photograph shows deputy sheriff Jagit Singh (*center*) receiving an award from the sheriff of Sutter County (*right*) at the 2005 Punjabi American Festival in Yuba City, California.

The arrival of South Asian students in the United States during the early twentieth century played an important role in unifying all immigrants from the Indian subcontinent. The young Indians from the middle and upper classes had little in common with the Punjabis who worked in the rural farmlands. Yet, in the eyes of white Americans, the students, too, were "Asian immigrants" and were often targets of the same prejudice as the Punjabis.

Building Unity

The social and legal discrimination the students experienced united them with rural Indian Americans. It was not unusual during the early 1900s for students to spend their summers working with Punjabis in the fields. In India, this interaction would have been unlikely because

"In those days the picture of India which most of the American people carried in their minds had little basis in reality. It was a confused jumble of yogis, snake charmers, and maharajas."

Dalip Singh Saund, who came to the United States to attend college, writing in his autobiography Congressman from India, *1960*

of caste separations and social custom. In addition, most Indians considered themselves citizens of their states—Punjab, Bengal, Bihar, and others—rather than of a unified country. In many cases, they spoke different native languages, such as Punjabi, Urdu, Hindi, or Bengali. Above all, they were of different faiths.

South Asian Americans, however, began to ignore the religious differences and class barriers that were so important in South Asia. The early interactions among all South Asian immigrants helped build a unity that overcame traditional differences. This unity still exists in the South Asian American community today.

The Gadar Party

In 1913, a group of South Asian Americans founded a political organization that welcomed all South Asian immigrants. It was known as the Gadar Party. Gadar, which means revolt, was dedicated to gaining independence from British rule for India.

▲ A group of South Asian students at the University of California at Berkeley gathers for a photograph during a visit by Bengali poet and spiritual leader Rabindranath Tagore (center). Some students who came in the early 1900s stayed to make their home in the United States; others returned to India.

The party also campaigned in the United States for the rights of South Asian Americans.

The Gadar Party published a weekly newspaper in several South Asian languages. The party also made a point of selecting leaders from the three main South Asian religions—Sikh, Hindu, and Muslim. In 1914, men representing the three faiths toured South Asian American communities, speaking out for independence from Britain. Gadar built a great deal of support among South Asian Americans by the 1930s.

Student, Farmer, Congressman

During the period when U.S. immigration from India was banned, groups such as the India League and the All-India Muslim League put pressure on U.S. lawmakers to allow South Asian Americans to become naturalized citizens. One of the leaders of this effort was Dr. Dalip Singh Saund (1899–1973), who had immigrated to the United States from Punjab in 1919 to attend college. Saund received a doctorate degree in mathematics in 1924, but he was unable to find a teaching job due to anti-immigrant prejudice.

▲ This photograph of Dalip Singh Saund was taken in the 1950s, when he became a U.S. Congressman.

Like other Punjabi Americans, Saund decided to farm, and he became a prosperous farmer in the Imperial Valley of California. In 1940, Saund founded the Indian Association of America to help change U.S. immigration laws and make South Asian Americans eligible for citizenship. Saund's group joined with the India League as well as with the India Welfare League, led by Muslim Mubarak Ali Khan, to work for fair treatment of South Asian Americans. In 1956, Saund became the first South Asian American elected to the U.S. Congress.

Work and Communities

▲ New York City has a large South Asian American population dating back to the 1960s. These dancers are getting ready to perform in the 2004 India Independence Day parade on New York's Madison Avenue.

The Punjabi farmers and other Indian Americans of the early 1900s are considered the pioneers of South Asian immigration to the United States. The more recent story of South Asian Americans involves hundreds of thousands of immigrants and very different experiences. The story began in 1965, when a change in U.S. immigration laws, combined with a demand for skilled workers, opened the door to South Asians.

Health Care Professionals

During the 1960s, there was an increased need for doctors and other medical professionals in the United States. The need arose because, in 1965, Congress created Medicare and Medicaid, national programs that provide health care for elderly Americans and for Americans living in poverty. The programs placed great demands on American hospitals and on health care workers.

The timing helped South Asians. A shortage of doctors in the United States arose at the same time that there was a surplus of trained doctors in both India and Pakistan. As a result, thousands of doctors came to the United States from South Asia—mainly from India—between 1968 and 1980. Researchers, engineers, and other highly educated professionals whose skills were in demand also entered the country in the same period.

The contribution of South Asian Americans to health care in the United States was enormous. Many South Asian doctors took jobs in city hospitals located in poor neighborhoods. In some cities— including New York City, Chicago, Illinois, and Houston, Texas— South Asian Americans continue to make up as much as 40 percent of doctors and 50 percent of the nurses on the staff of hospitals.

The Concert for Bangladesh

In the spring of 1971, the violent war for the independence of Bangladesh was at its height. One of the most well known Bengalis in the world was the classical sitar player, Ravi Shankar. That year, in an effort to help his people, Shankar approached George Harrison, a former member of the Beatles. Shankar and Harrison arranged a concert to raise funds for refugees from Bangladesh. In August 1971, the Concert for Bangladesh was held at Madison Square Garden in New York City and attended by more than forty thousand people. Shankar, a Bengali Hindu, played with a group that included Ali Akbar Khan and Alla Rakha,

▲ Bengali musician Ravi Shankar plays his sitar at the Monterey, California, pop festival in 1967. Shankar has since made his home in California.

Bengali Muslims. Harrison followed and was joined by several American and British pop and rock stars of the day. The concert was a historic occasion, being the first large musical event to raise money for an international cause.

Settling in the Cities

After 1965, South Asian Americans established communities all over the United States. Because most immigrants had lived in cities on the Indian subcontinent, they settled in U.S. cities. While Indians, Pakistanis, Bangladeshis, and Sri Lankans did not always live in the same neighborhoods, they almost always settled near each other.

New York City is a typical example of the pattern. In the 1970s, immigrants from India settled in Jackson Heights, a neighborhood in the borough of Queens in New York City. There, the first neighborhood known as a "Little India" developed. It was normal to see Sikhs wearing turbans and women wearing saris on the main street. The borough bordering Queens is Brooklyn, and in the late 1970s, Pakistani Americans settled there. On many streets, stores and restaurants began to display window signs in Urdu, the main language of Pakistan.

The largest and most crowded borough of New York City is Manhattan, across the East River from Queens and Brooklyn. There, more recent arrivals from Bangladesh and Sri Lanka have settled in and opened stores, auto workshops, and other small businesses. All of these South Asian American people live within a few miles of one another.

> "For the first few years I had nothing . . . I could hardly afford French fries. But I made a go for myself. It's the chance for success that attracts people like me."
>
> *Rahaul Merchant, who came to the United States from India in 1979, earned college degrees in computer science and business, and is now an executive at a financial investment company in New York City, 1997*

◀ Boxes of relief supplies for Sri Lankan tsunami victims are stacked in front of a statue of Buddha at a Sri Lankan American temple in Queens in New York City. Many Sri Lankan immigrants have settled near other South Asian Americans in and around New York City.

Most of the people in these communities, especially the younger generations, call themselves desis.

By the mid-1980s, thousands of the middle-class immigrants who had come to the United States from South Asia had settled in urban areas. About 60 percent of them had become naturalized

Devon Avenue

One South Asian American community developed rapidly in the 1970s in Chicago, Illinois. The area of the city around Devon Avenue became known as "Little India." As immigrants from Pakistan began to arrive in the neighborhood, the area became what some people called an "Indo-Pak" community.

At first, some of the tensions that existed between India and Pakistan and between their two main religions—Hinduism and Islam—surfaced on Devon Avenue. Independence Day for each country is one day apart—August 14 for Pakistan and August 15 for India. This meant that two separate parades were held each year on two successive days. Politics surfaced in other ways when Indian Americans requested that a street be renamed Gandhi Way, after Mahatma Gandhi, founder of modern India. Pakistani Americans responded by requesting that a nearby street be named Muhammad Ali Jinnah Way, in honor of the founder of Pakistan. The neighborhood soon had streets named after each national hero.

Today, Hindu temples can be found near Muslim mosques and Sikh gurdwaras. In the Devon Avenue community, residents respect and, in some cases, observe all South Asian holidays. Other cultural traditions have been main-

tained, too. In Pakistani restaurants, there is no pork served because of Muslim religious law. No beef is served in Hindu Indian restaurants for the same reason. All South Asian restaurants in the neighborhood, however, feature many vegetarian dishes that form an important part of the diet in South Asia.

▲ Many South Asian Americans live in Chicago's multiethnic Devon Avenue neighborhood.

▲ Sikh American boys study at their temple in New Jersey. The boys will retain a sense of their South Asian heritage as they grow up in U.S. society.

citizens. These new citizens were able to use the rules of the 1965 Immigration Act to sponsor relatives to come to the United States.

Adjusting to U.S. Society

Despite growing acceptance of their culture in the United States, many South Asians faced a difficult adjustment when they immigrated. As eager as many were to leave behind the strict class divisions and roles, South Asian Americans wanted to retain some values from their native homelands.

South Asian American women who attempted to work as well as care for their families in the traditional way often faced difficulties. In South Asia, all domestic chores were the responsibility of women. Usually, young married women could expect help from older female relatives. Immigrant couples in the United States, however, did not always have close older relatives. In many cases, both husband and wife worked long hours at their jobs and found it difficult to raise their children in the religious and social traditions they themselves had experienced.

Changing and Maintaining Traditions

The children of immigrants grew up American and often adopted clothing styles, language, and behavior that were far outside South Asian traditions. In South Asia, young people were encouraged to marry only partners approved by their parents, usually people from the same region or social class. In the United States, younger South

A South Asian American Family

Malavika Shrikhande was born in Mumbai, India, in 1967 and arrived in United States in 1999. She has an M.A. in history and a B.A. in library science. Malavika became a U.S. citizen in 2003. Her husband Devendra, a professional photographer who had lived in the United States since 1986, had decided he wanted to marry someone who had an Indian upbringing like his own. The couple's two families met in India through a traditional matchmaking process; Devendra made a trip to India to meet Malavika, and the two decided to marry.

When Malavika arrived in the United States in 1999, she was struck first by the freezing winter weather, then by the unusual friendliness of people to strangers. She had grown up in a large, crowded city and had arrived to make her home in a small town in Wyoming, the least populated state in the United States. Although they were friendly, the people were hard to find. "Where is everyone?" she asked when she saw streets with nobody on the sidewalks.

This photo shows the Shrikhande family in 2005.

Malavika and her husband are both proficient in computer technology. In 2000, they started a web design and marketing business, which they continue to run as partners. They have a young daughter, Maitreyi. Although Maitreyi's parents will teach her their language, values, and spiritual beliefs, Maitreyi's mother says she will grow up as an American.

The Shrikhandes eat fewer traditional Indian foods than when Malavika first arrived, but they continue to celebrate Divali and other Hindu holidays. They also maintain a strong connection with their families in India—Malavika and her mother communicate regularly with webcams set up in their homes.

Asian Americans met all kinds of people from many different backgrounds, and they were not necessarily willing to follow traditional routes to marriage.

Many South Asian Americans tried to reaffirm their heritage by attending the local temples and mosques that were established by the hundreds in cities across the country. Community centers were also established to teach native languages as well as traditional music and dances. In New York City alone, more than one hundred such cultural organizations arose between 1968 and 1975.

Small Businesses and Service Industries

Most of the South Asians who immigrated to the U.S. between 1965 and the mid-1980s were educated, middle-class professional people from India or Pakistan. They were one of the most successful immigrant groups to come to the United States in the twentieth century.

Immigrants after 1985 were generally without the professional qualifications that marked the earlier immigrants. The newcomers,

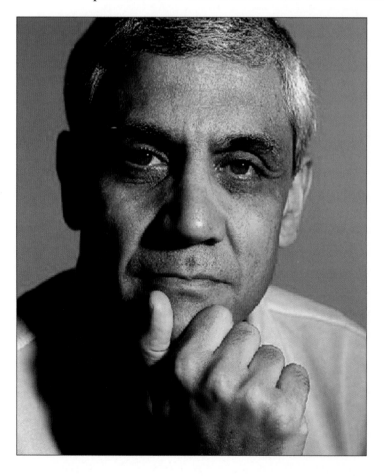

who came from Sri Lanka or Bangladesh as well as from India and Pakistan, were more likely to find jobs in service industries or become small business owners. Although the desire to succeed in the United States remained powerful among new immigrants, opportunities for financial success were fewer. Jobs in

◀ Born in India, Vinod Khosla was cofounder of Sun Microsystems and is still a leading figure among the computer industries based in Silicon Valley, California. Many South Asian Americans have found success in the field of new technology.

▲ Sikh taxi drivers gather at work in New York City. South Asian Americans drive more than half of all taxi cabs in the city.

health care and business were not as plentiful as they had been in previous decades.

This fact, however, did not deter South Asian Americans from hard work and enterprise. By the 1990s, thousands of South Asians were working as cabdrivers, in newsstands, and in gas stations and convenience stores.

Other South Asian Americans turned to establishing or buying small businesses. Today, these Americans own and operate 300 of New York City's 330 street newsstands. In Chicago, Illinois, Indian and Pakistani Americans own about 90 percent of the shops in a large national doughnut franchise.

Working Together

Young men from Bangladesh or Sri Lanka live together to share expenses and responsibilities, much as the Punjabis did in the early 1900s. In New York City, which has thousands of South Asian American taxi drivers, a group of men may pool their money to make a down payment on a taxi. The partners can then take different shifts and drive the cab around the clock. Once the cab is paid off, they may decide to open a business or move into some other area of work. In Manhattan, for example, Pakistani Americans and Indian Americans run dozens of small auto repair shops and taxi garages. "Four drivers making $30,000 a year will get together and buy a $100,000 workshop," explains Farooq Bhatti, a naturalized citizen from Pakistan. "In Pakistan, we are very good at repairing cars, because parts are so expensive."

Regional Occupations

Immigrants from certain regions of South Asia followed one another into specific occupations or businesses. Bangladeshis worked as cooks in many Indian restaurants. Punjabi Sikhs often ran gas stations. Many Sri Lankans become involved in video rental stores.

Perhaps the most visible occupation of South Asian Americans has been the ownership of hotels and economy motels by people originally from the Indian state of Gujarat. In many cases, the Gujaratis have the last name Patel, a common surname in that region. Motels became attractive employment opportunities because they allowed extended families to live and work together. According to the Hotel Owners' Association of America, South Asian Americans operate about twenty thousand hotels in the United States today, about 37 percent of the industry. In addition, South Asian Americans own and operate more than half of all budget motels in the United States.

The September 11 Attacks

The successful experience of South Asians in the United States has been overshadowed in recent years by events following the terrorist attacks on September 11, 2001. The attacks killed almost three thousand people in New York City and Washington, D.C. Among the many victims were South Asian Americans.

> "For every person who thinks I'm smarter and better, there's someone who thinks . . . I'm about to blow up a building."
>
> *Nisha Ganatra,*
> *a South Asian*
> *American, 2004*

The attacks on the United States were tragic for all U.S. citizens. Unfortunately, some turned their sorrow into hatred and began to lash out at people from ethnic groups they associated with the attacks. When news reports stated that the attacks had been carried out by Muslim extremists under orders from Arab terrorist leader Osama bin Laden, Muslims in the United States became targets. "After 9/11, says Dr. Tamina Begum, a Muslim who immigrated to

▲ Muslim Americans worship at the Islamic Cultural Center of New York a few days after the September 11 attacks in 2001. The mosque's leader denounced the attacks, saying, "Such inhuman acts are directed against all humanity, against civilization, against freedom."

New York City from Bangladesh in 1995, "I could not leave my home for two months without being harassed."

Because Osama Bin Laden was believed to be in hiding in Afghanistan, a few U.S. citizens lashed out at people they associated with that region—including South Asians. To some Americans, Sikhs resembled Afghanis, due to their turbans and their dark skin color, and Sikhs were among the first victims of hate crimes. On September 15, 2001, a Sikh gas station owner in Arizona, Balbir Singh Sodhi, was shot to death by a man who told witnesses he planned to kill "Arabs." On October 4, 2001, another American, Vaudev Patel, was shot behind the counter of his gas station in Mesquite, Texas. A Pakistani restaurant in Salt Lake City, Utah, was burned down at about the same time. In the six months following September 11, the FBI began investigating more than three hundred hate crimes against Arab, Muslim, and South Asian Americans.

CHAPTER 6

South Asian Americans in U.S. Society

Today, as in the past, the great majority of South Asian Americans—more than 2 million of them—are of Indian descent. There are about 300,000 Pakistani Americans, comprising slightly more than 10 percent of the South Asian American population. Bangladeshi Americans (about 90,000) and Sri Lankan Americans (about 30,000) together make up less than 5 percent of the South Asian population in the United States.

A Successful Presence

In many ways, South Asian Americans have been among the most successful immigrant groups to come to the United States in the twentieth century. The average family income of South Asian Americans is about $60,000 per year—higher than the national average of about $39,000. About half of the South Asian

▼ Indian restaurants line the street in the Little India section of Greenwich Village, a neighborhood in New York City.

▲ Ranbir Kaur (*center*) of the U.S. Army plays cards with her father (*left*) and her grandfather (*right*) in 2005. Ranbir's family immigrated from Punjab in 1993, when she was a child. Ranbir is at home in her traditional Sikh household, but she is thoroughly American in her chosen career with the U.S. military.

Americans now living in the United States are college graduates. Although South Asian Americans make up less than 1 percent of the U.S. population, they make up more than 5 percent of the scientists, engineers, and computer specialists in the United States.

At the same time, a great deal of South Asian culture has entered American daily life. The popular South Asian music *bhangra*, which is based on Punjabi folk music, can be heard in nightclubs around the United States and on television shows. South Asian foods and spices are commonly found in American stores. Words from South Asian languages—including yoga, guru, curry, and others—are part of everyday American English.

ABCDs

Many older South Asian Americans try to hold onto religious observances, traditional languages, and cultural heritage as they raise their children. The children, however, grow up in both South Asian and U.S. cultures. An estimated 30 percent of U.S.-raised South Asian Americans marry someone of a different heritage. For young South Asian Americans, the pressure to be part of two cultures is overwhelming. It is such a common condition that a term is used to describe these young people—ABCDs. It stands for American-Born Confused Desis. A U.S.-born college student of Pakistani descent describes her confusion: "I was born here, went to school here. I have never lived in Pakistan for any length of time—I can barely utter a few words of Urdu. I have been brought up as an

Celebrating Holidays

As South Asian American communities have grown, the celebration of religious holidays has helped to bring those communities together. For Muslim Americans, the most important holiday is Eid al-Fitr, the night that marks the end of the month-long fasting period of Ramadan. For Hindu Americans, Diwali—the festival of lights— remains the most important holiday. Sri Lankan Americans, most of them Buddhists, celebrate the Sinhalese New Year and the Buddhist festival of Vesak.

"I was approached by an employee of the club who told [me] I wouldn't be allowed in unless I removed my turban. I explained that it is an article of my faith and I couldn't. My parents emigrated here from India in 1970. I was born and raised in the United States. I'm tired of being treated like a second-class citizen just because I have a different appearance."

Dr. Harpreet Grewal, a Sikh, who was in medical school in Pittsburgh, Pennsylvania, when he was denied entry to a nightclub, 2003

American, but Americans call me an Asian and do not fully identify with me. My Pakistani cousins consider me an American. That is why I call myself an American-Born Confused Desi. I am not comfortable in my own skin. I do not know which place to call my home."

Continuing Unease

While the contributions of South Asian Americans are widely acknowledged, a wave of prejudice has arisen in the first decade of the twenty-first century. The hate crimes associated with the September 11 attacks diminished after several months, but many South Asian Americans in the United States remain uneasy. People responsible for the crimes have been tried and sentenced in court, but South Asian Americans claim that prejudice against South Asians has not diminished. They point to the fact that the U.S. government passed legislation in 2002 that required non-naturalized men and boys from Muslim countries—including Pakistan and Bangladesh—to register at local immigration offices. More than eighty thousand Muslims registered, including about twenty thousand Pakistanis and Bangladeshis. None of these people was charged with terrorist crimes.

Another element of the anti-immigrant attitude against South Asian Americans stems from the concern that they are taking jobs

> "I think it is absolutely the strength of America. . . . This is a country where people are judged on their ability and their performance. I think that is very important. What makes the American system so successful is the fact that immigrants and their children born here can get ahead, can do very well, with hard work."
>
> *U.S. Congressman from Louisiana Bobby Jindal, 2004*

▲ Before being elected to Congress, Bobby Jindal ran for governor in the state of Louisiana. He was photographed in New Orleans with his wife and daughter during his 2003 campaign.

from other American workers, a common anti-immigrant complaint throughout U.S. history. Many of the job-related concerns stem from the South Asians who come to work in the United States on H-1B visas. Although there is no firm evidence to support it, some Americans who work in technology fields claim that they are being replaced by H-1B workers who are paid lower wages.

A Hopeful Future

Despite the events of recent years, South Asian Americans remain a vital part of U.S. life. Many American political leaders have spoken out against intolerance and religious discrimination shown toward South Asian Americans. The promise and opportunity that has drawn South Asians to the United States for more than a century still remains a powerful attraction. South Asian Americans will continue to make important contributions to the lives of all Americans.

One encouraging example is the 2004 election of Bobby Jindal from Louisiana to the U.S. House of Representatives. Jindal became the first South Asian American elected to Congress in nearly fifty years. Jindal, who was born in the United States after his parents came from India in the late 1960s, won more than 75 percent of the vote in a district whose majority is white and conservative. His relatives in Punjab danced in the streets and distributed candy when word of his election reached the small town from which his parents emigrated. Jindal says that his success comes from the fact that the United States is, and always has been, a country of opportunity.

Notable South Asian Americans

Amar Bose (1929–) U.S.-born son of Bengali immigrants who founded the Bose Corporation, a leading maker of sound systems.

Kalpana Chawla (1961–2003) Indian-born physicist and aerospace engineer who died in the explosion of the Space Shuttle *Columbia.*

Chitra Banerjee Divakaruni (1957–) Indian-born novelist, poet, and professor at the University of Houston.

Sanjay Gupta (1957–) Indian-born surgeon and health reporter for CNN.

Zakir Hussain (1951–) Indian-born Muslim who is a world renowned tabla player and a visiting professor at Princeton University in New Jersey.

Muhammed Zafar Iqbal (1952–) Bangladeshi-born physicist and science fiction author.

Bobby Jindal (1971–) U.S.-born Congressman of Punjabi heritage.

Norah Jones (1979–) U.S.-born singer and daughter of Bengali Ravi Shankar.

Fazlur Rahman Khan (1929–1982) Bangladeshi-born engineer who designed Chicago's Sears Tower, the tallest building in the United States.

Har Gobind Khorana (1922–) professor at the University of Wisconsin who was born in what is now Pakistan and won the Nobel Prize for Medicine in 1967 for his work in genetics.

Zubin Mehta (1936–) Indian-born conductor who served as music director of the New York Philharmonic Orchestra from 1978 to 1991.

Ismail Merchant (1936–2005) Indian-born movie producer who attended college in New York City and became one of the world's most successful independent movie makers.

Bharati Mukherjee (1940–) Bengali-born novelist and professor of English whose novels explore the multicultural identity of Americans today.

Walpola Rahula (1911–1998) Sri Lankan-born Buddhist monk who became the first Buddhist monk ever to hold a professorship in the United States, at Northwestern University.

Dalip Singh Saund (1899–1973) Indian-born mathematician and farmer who became the first South Asian American elected to the U.S. Congress.

Fareed Zakaria (1964–) Indian-born Muslim who became a journalist, magazine editor, and TV presenter.

Time Line

1885   Indian National Congress (INC) is founded.

1899   First wave of South Asian immigration to the United States begins.

1905   Asiatic Exclusion League (AEL) is formed in San Francisco.

1906   Muslim League is founded.

1907   Bellingham Riots drive South Asian Americans from Bellingham, Washington.

1908   Canada bans South Asian immigration.

1913   California passes Alien Land Law; Gadar Party is founded.

1917   Immigration Act of 1917 prohibits immigration from nations including India and imposes a literacy test on immigrants.

1923   In *United States vs. Bhagat Singh Thind*, the Supreme Court rules that Indians cannot become naturalized U.S. citizens.

1924   Immigration Act of 1924 (also known as the National Origins Act) further restricts Asian immigration.

1946   Luce-Cellar Act is signed.

1947   India gains independence from Britain, and the nation of Pakistan is created from parts of India; second wave of South Asian immigration to the United States begins.

1948   British island colony of Ceylon is granted independence.

1956   Dalip Singh Saund is elected to U.S. Congress from California; California Alien Land Law is repealed.

1965   Immigration and Nationality Act is passed by Congress; Medicare and Medicaid programs create demand for healthcare workers; third wave of South Asian immigration to the United States begins.

1971   East Pakistan becomes the nation of Bangladesh.

1972   Ceylon becomes the Republic of Sri Lanka.

1983   Civil war begins in Sri Lanka.

1990   Immigration Reform and Control Act increases the total U.S. immigration quota to 700,000 per year and introduces H1-B visas.

2001   September 11: Terrorists attack World Trade Center in New York City and Pentagon in Washington, D.C., spurring hate crimes against Muslims, Arabs, and South Asians in the United States.

2004   Bobby Jindal is elected to U.S. Congress from Louisiana.

Glossary

alien person living in a nation other than his or her birth nation and who has not become a citizen of his or her new nation of residence

borough district of a city or a state

caste social ranking in Hindu society

Caucasian term used to define people whose ancestors came from Europe, North Africa, West Asia, South Asia, and parts of Central Asia. It is also used to mean people with light-colored skin.

census official population count

colony nation, territory, or people under the control of another country

culture language, beliefs, customs, and ways of life shared by a group of people from the same region or nation

deported officially sent out of a country

desi term used by South Asian Americans to describe one of their own group

discrimination treatment of one group or person differently from another

drought prolonged period without rain

emigrate leave one nation or region to go and live in another place

ethnic having certain racial, national, tribal, religious, or cultural origins

heritage something handed down from previous generations

immigrant person who arrives in a new nation or region to take up residence

lease acquire the right to a piece of land under a contract for a set period of time

migrant moving from place to place

according to the seasons, for work opportunities, or for other reasons

naturalization process of becoming a citizen by living in the United States for a number of years and passing a citizenship test

plantation large farm that grows primarily one crop, such as sugarcane, cotton, or tea

prejudice bias against or dislike of a person or group because of race, nationality, or other factors

quota assigned proportion; in the case of immigration, a limit on the number of immigrants allowed from a particular country

refugee person who leaves a country or region because of conflict, natural disaster, or persecution

sari dress formed from a length of cloth wrapped around a body

service industry area of work that provides services instead of products; service businesses include banks, entertainment, food service, tourism, and health care, among many others

sponsor put someone's name forward and take responsibility for them

subcontinent large and distinct part of a continent (the Indian subcontinent is part of the continent of Asia)

turban head covering formed from a length of cloth wound around the head

visa document that permits a person to enter a nation for a set period of time

yoga form of exercise derived from the Hindu religion

Further Resources

Books

Ingram, Scott. *The Indian Americans.* Immigrants in America (series). Lucent Books, 2003.

Leonard, Karen Isaksen. *The South Asian Americans.* The New Americans (series). Greenwood Press, 1997.

Natividad, Irene and Susan B. Gall (editors). *The Asian American Almanac.* Asian American Reference Library (series). U.X.L./Gale, 2003.

Wilkinson, Ian. *Gandhi: The Young Protestor Who Founded a Nation.* World History Biographies (series). National Geographic Chidren's Books, 2005.

Web Sites

Echoes of Freedom
www.lib.berkeley.edu/SSEAL/echoes/toc.html
History of South Asians in California from the University of California

PBS—Roots in the Sand
www.pbs.org/rootsinthesand/index.html
Portrait of pioneering Punjabi-Mexicans, taken from a television documentary

Publisher's note to educators and parents: Our editors have carefully reviewed these Web sites to ensure that they are suitable for children. Many Web sites change frequently, however, and we cannot guarantee that a site's future contents will continue to meet our high standards of quality and educational value. Be advised that children should be closely supervised whenever they access the Internet.

Where to Visit

Angel Island State Park
Angel Island
Belvedere-Tiburon, CA 94920
Telephone: (415) 435-1915
www.angelisland.org

About the Author

Scott Ingram is the author of more than fifty books for young adults. In 2004, he won the NAACP Image Award for an outstanding literary work for children for his book about the Civil Rights March of 1963, published by World Almanac® Library in its *Landmark Events in American History* series. Ingram lives in Portland, Connecticut.

Index